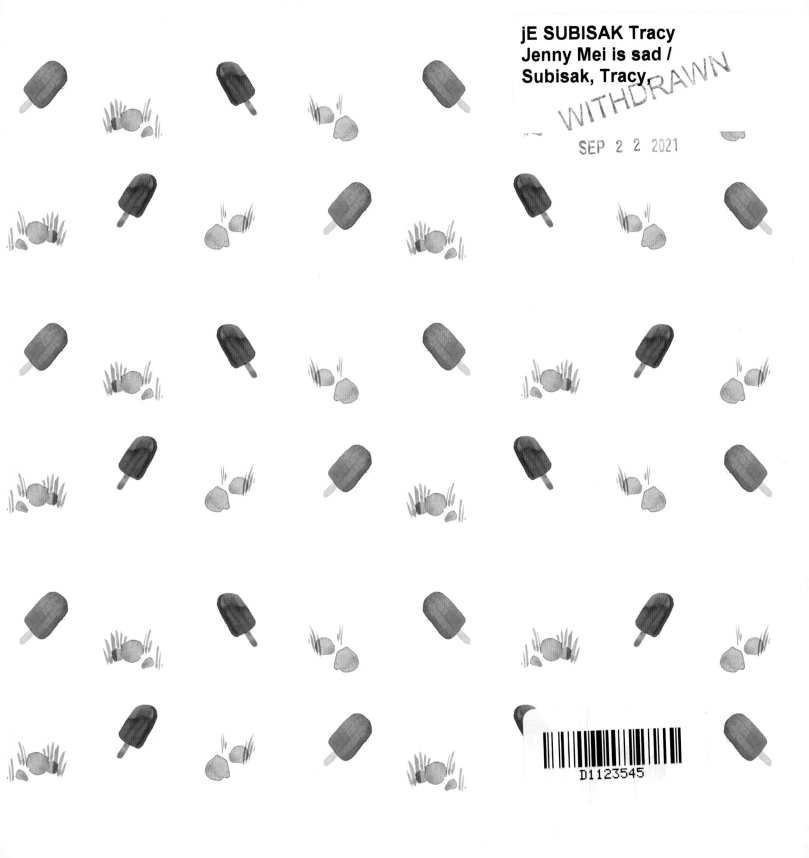

# Jenny Mei Is Sad

Tracy Subisak

**L B**
Little, Brown and Company
New York  Boston

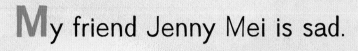

My friend Jenny Mei is sad.

But you might not
be able to tell.

Even when she's sad, she still smiles

and shares her orange with Harold

and admires
Izzy's drawings.

And she really likes to make everyone laugh.

But some days are not as fun . . .

Today is one of those days . . .

and on those
days I wait.

Jenny Mei says that Ms. Abbott is a good listener.

She says I'm a good listener too,
but today is a quiet walk home.

What we need are . . .

Popsicles.

And kick
    the rock.

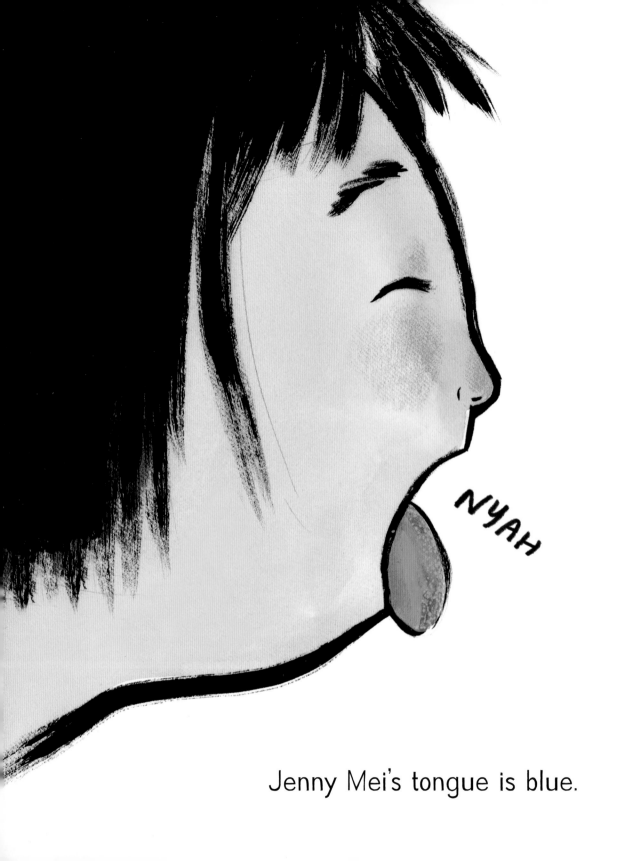

Jenny Mei's tongue is blue.

UNNGHHHH

Mine is purple.

I ask Jenny Mei,

How are you doing?

She doesn't answer.

Being sad is hard.

Jenny Mei is sad.

But she knows I'm here

for fun and not-fun and
everything in between.

Because that's what
friends are for.

To Matty
for being there through fun and not-fun
and everything in between

## About This Book

The illustrations for this book were done in India ink, Japanese watercolor, pastel, and colored pencil on Fabriano Artistico watercolor paper. This book was edited by Alvina Ling and designed by Véronique Lefèvre Sweet. The production was supervised by Patricia Alvarado, and the production editor was Annie McDonnell. The text was set in Absent Grotesque, and the display type is the author's hand lettering.

Hachette Book Group, Inc. • The publisher is not responsible for websites (or their content) that are not owned by the publisher. • Library of Congress Cataloging-in-Publication Data • Names: Subisak, Tracy, author. • Title: Jenny Mei is sad / by Tracy Subisak. • Description: First edition. | New York : Little, Brown and Company, 2021. | Audience: Ages 4-8. | Summary: "A picture book about sadness uniquely told from the friend's point of view as she does her best to comfort her friend Jenny Mei"— Provided by publisher. • Identifiers: LCCN 2019055173 | ISBN: 978-0-316-53771-1 (hardcover) • Subjects: CYAC: Sadness–Fiction. | Friendship–Fiction. • Classification: LCC PZ7.1.S825 Jen 2021 | DDC [E] –dc23 • LC record available at https://lccn.loc.gov/2019055173 • ISBN: 978-0-316-53771-1 • PRINTED IN CHINA APS • 10 9 8 7 6 5 4 3 2 1

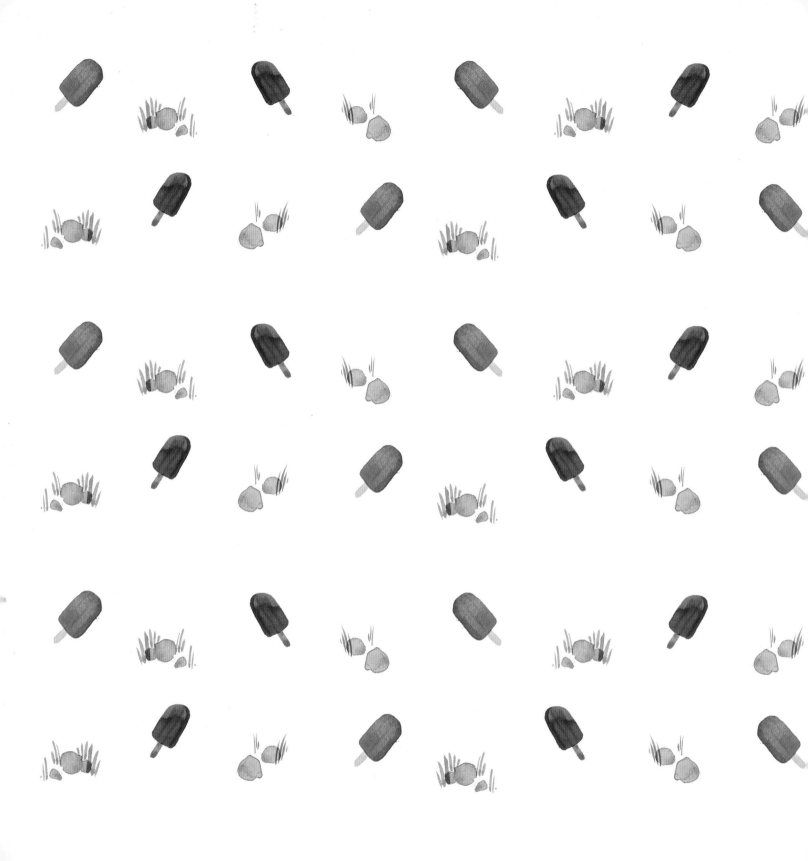